CHRISTMAS
COLORING BOOK

TRACE AND COLOR!

MERRY CHRISTMAS

COUNT WITH ME!

Count the items in each box and color the correct number!

4   1   3   2

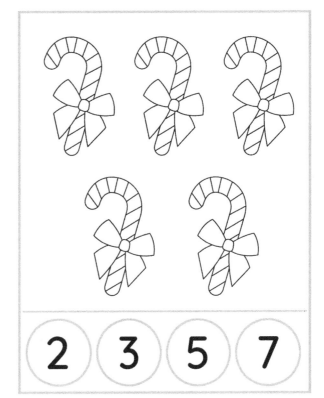

2   3   5   7

2   1   5   4

8   5   4   3

CONNECT THE DOTS

CHRISTMAS SYMMETRY

Finish the picture!

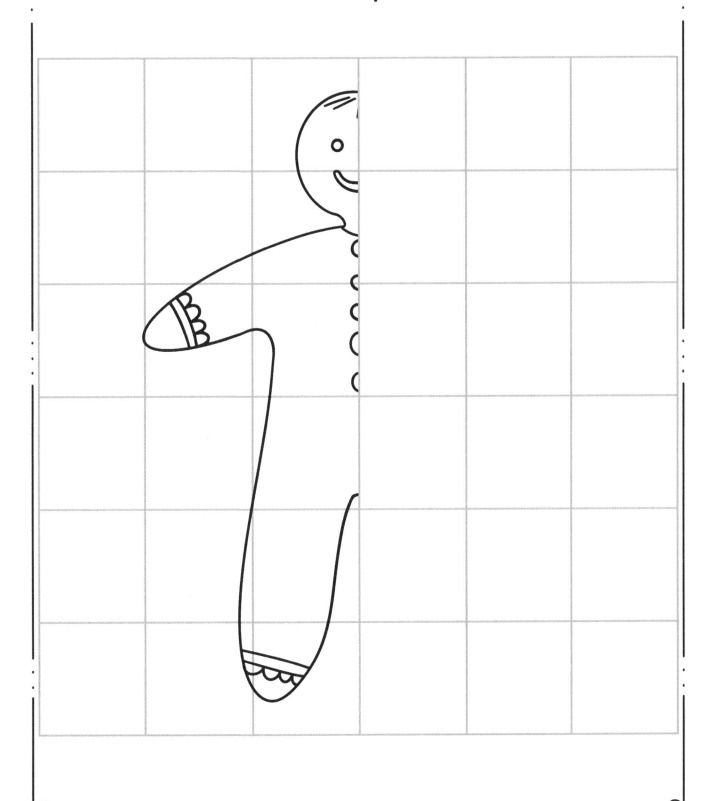

CHRISTMAS ABC

Fill in the missing letters and finish the alphabet.

OH CHRISTMAS TREE!

CHRISTMAS MAZE

START

FINISH

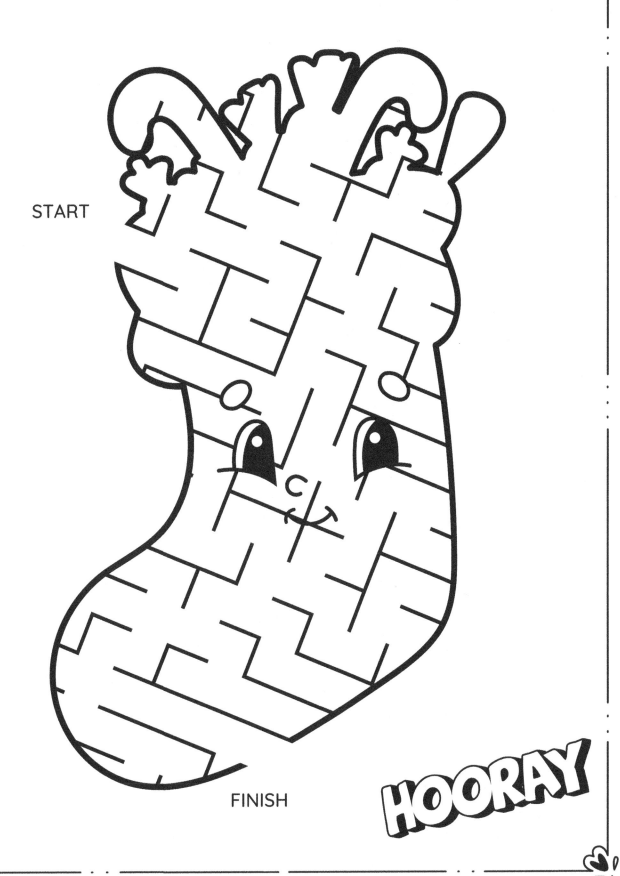

HOORAY

CONNECT
THE DOTS

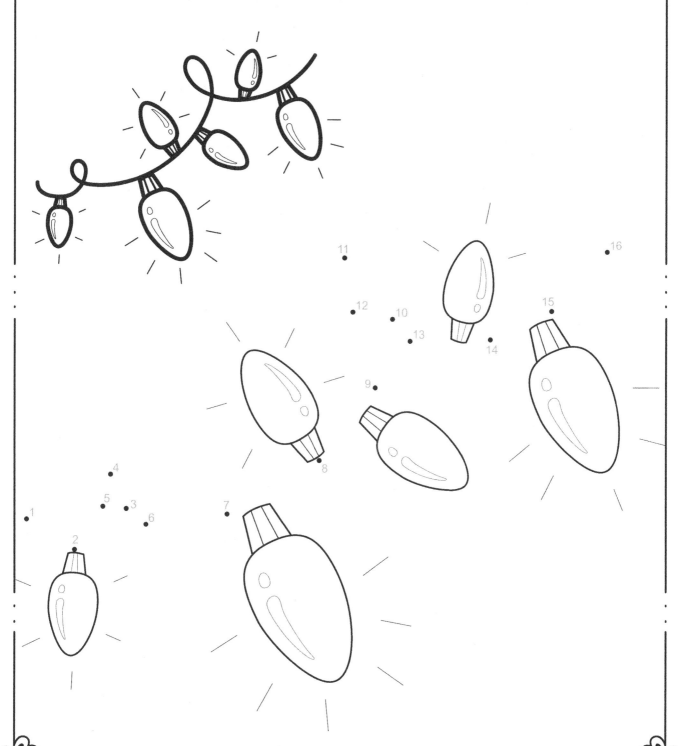

CHRISTMAS GREETINGS

TRACE AND COLOR!

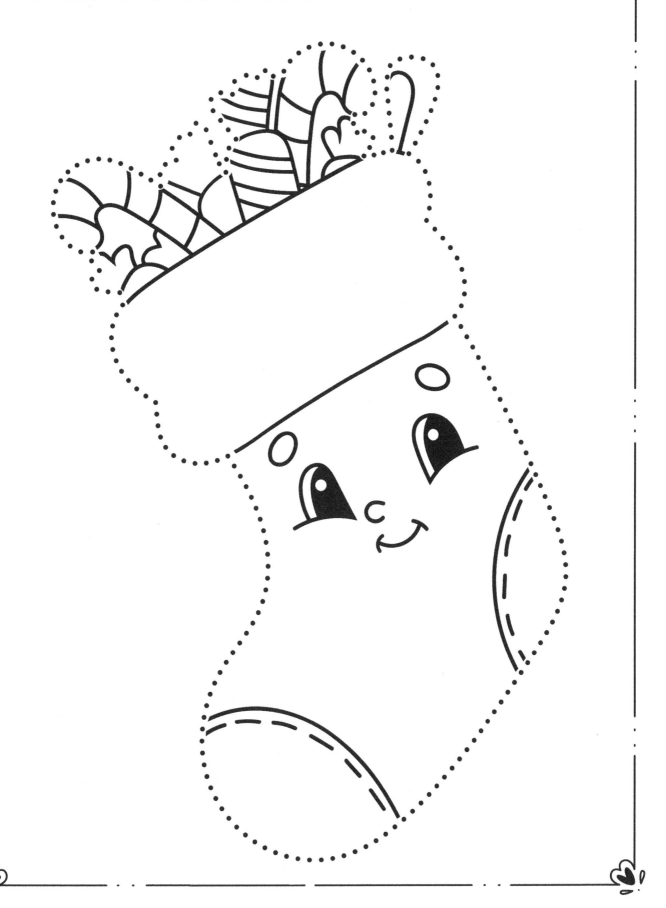

CHRISTMAS SYMMETRY

Finish the picture!

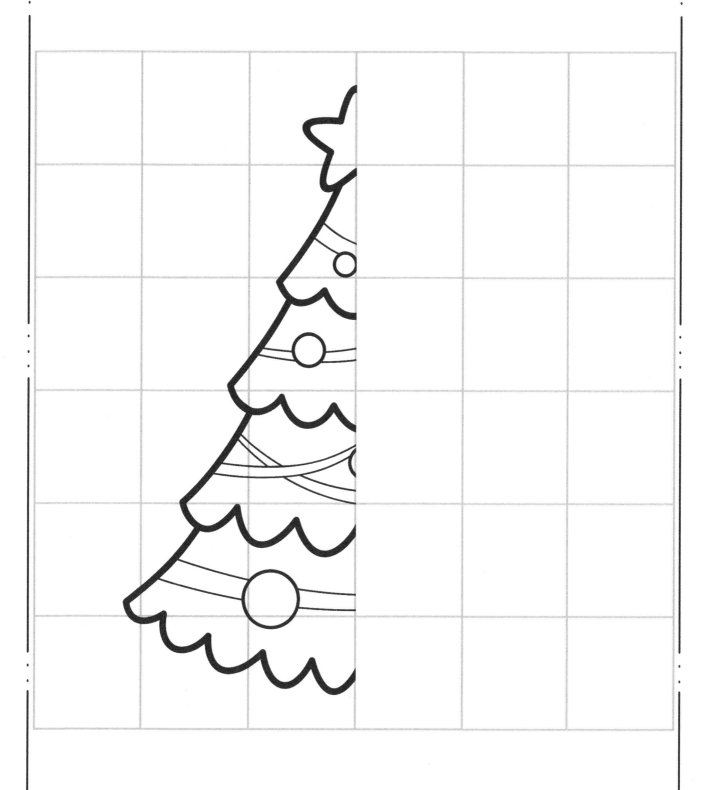

ALPHABET COLORING

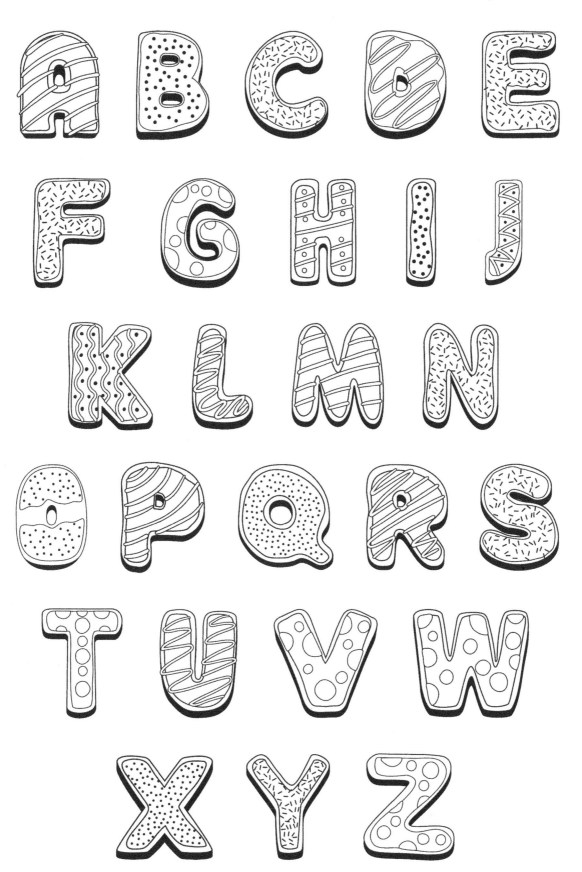

CHRISTMAS COUNTING

How many Christmas items do you count?
Write the number in the box!

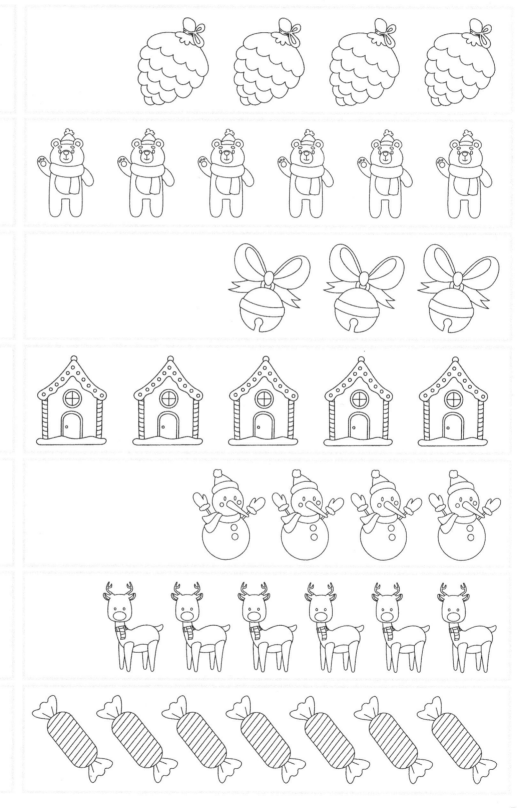

MERRY CHRISTMAS

CHRISTMAS SYMMETRY

Finish the picture!

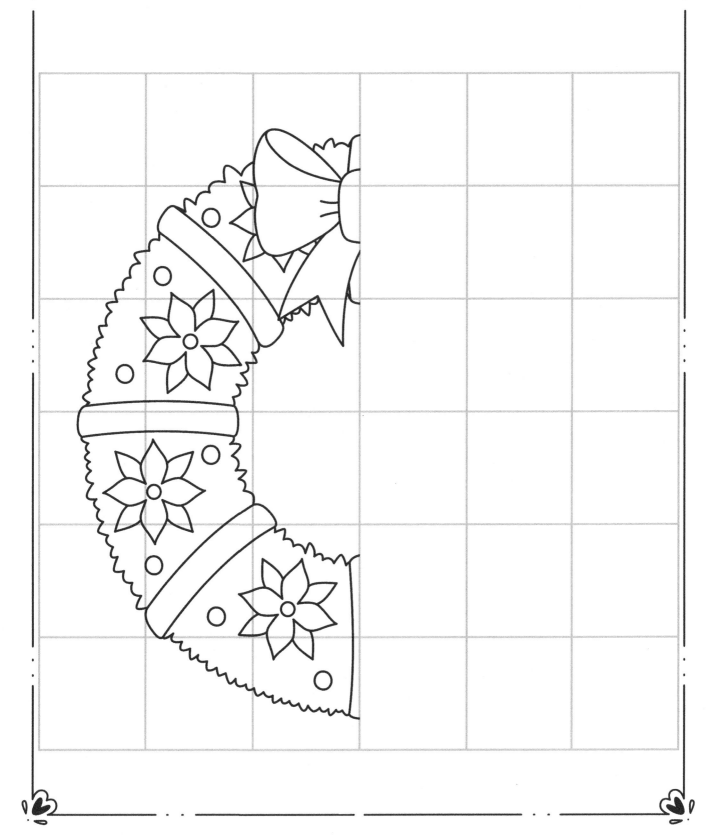

CHRISTMAS MAZE

START

FINISH

HO HO HO!

TRACE AND COLOR!

CHRISTMAS COUNTING

How many Christmas items do you count?
Write the number in the box!

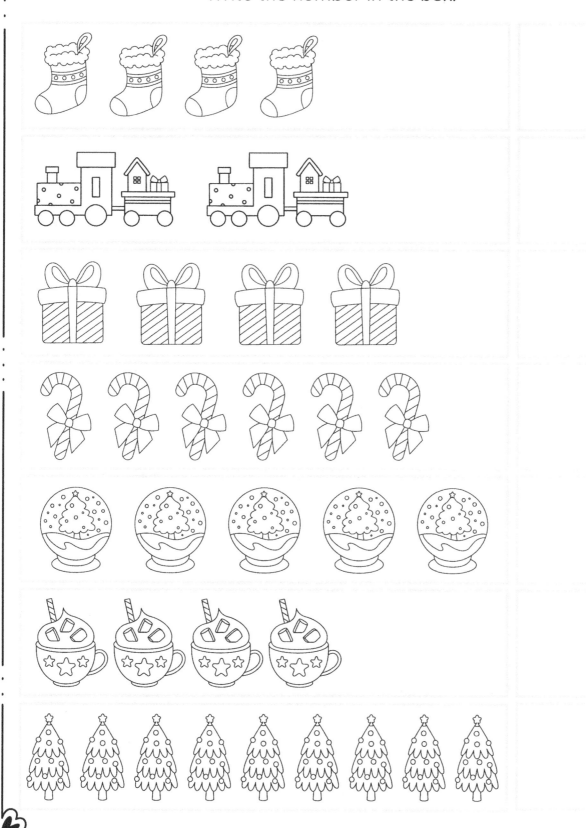

MERRY
Christmas
AND HAPPY NEW YEAR

Made in United States
Orlando, FL
14 December 2024

55700871R00057